The Case of the Fifth Word

"The four words will tell Davenport where the stolen jewelry is hidden!" Mrs. Brown said.

"Right," Encyclopedia said. "The code is simple."

"Leroy!" Mrs. Brown exclaimed. "What do the four words mean?"

"You already guessed, Mom. They tell where the jewelry is hidden."

Mrs. Brown looked ready to explode with impatience. "*Where?*"

Encyclopedia smiled. "Why, under the fifth word!"

WHAT WAS THE FIFTH WORD? AND HOW DID ENCYCLOPEDIA BROWN DISCOVER IT?

ENCYCLOPEDIA BROWN

and the Case of the Disgusting Sneakers

DONALD J. SOBOL

Illustrated by Gail Owens

A DELL YEARLING BOOK

35 Years of Exceptional Reading

Dell Yearling Books
Established 1966

Published by
Dell Yearling
an imprint of
Random House Children's Books
a division of Random House, Inc.
1540 Broadway
New York, New York 10036

Visit us on the Web! www.randomhouse.com/kids
Educators and librarians, for a variety of teaching tools, visit us at
www.randomhouse.com/teachers

ISBN: 0-553-15851-1

Printed in the United States of America

August 2002

30 29 28 27 26 25 24

OPM

For
Rose and Edward Dreyer

Contents

ENCYCLOPEDIA BROWN
and the Case of the Disgusting Sneakers

The Case of the Fifth Word

In Idaville, no one—grown-up or child—got away with breaking the law.

Police officers across the nation wondered how Idaville did it. What was the secret?

To passing motorists, Idaville looked like any other seaside town. It had playgrounds, banks, parking meters, and beautiful white beaches. It had churches, a synagogue, and two delicatessens.

And it had a fine new police station.

But the real headquarters for catching lawbreakers was a red brick house at 13

Rover Avenue. There lived ten-year-old Encyclopedia Brown, America's crime-buster in sneakers. No one except his parents knew that he was the mastermind behind the town's spotless police record.

Encyclopedia's father was chief of police. Everyone thought that he must be the smartest police chief in the country.

Chief Brown was smart and quick. He didn't sit around and worry. When he came up against a case he could not solve, he acted at once.

He cleared his desk, put on his hat, and went home to dinner.

Encyclopedia solved the case for him before the meal was over.

Chief Brown would have liked to tell everyone about his only child. But who would believe him? Who would believe the best detective alive was a fifth-grader?

So he said nothing.

Encyclopedia never spoke of the help he gave his father. He didn't want to seem different from other boys.

But there was nothing he could do about his nickname. He was stuck with it.

Only his parents and teachers called him

by his real name, Leroy. Everyone else called him Encyclopedia.

An encyclopedia is a book or set of books filled with facts from *A* to *Z*. So was Encyclopedia's head. He read more books than anyone in Idaville, and he never forgot a fact.

His pals said he was like a library and a computer rolled into one, and more user-friendly.

At the dinner table Tuesday night, Chief Brown stared at his cream of mushroom soup. Encyclopedia and his mother knew what *that* meant. He had a mystery he could not solve.

"Tim Nolan died yesterday," he announced matter-of-factly.

"That name is familiar," Mrs. Brown said. "Wasn't he mixed up in a jewelry robbery a few years ago?"

"Five years ago," Chief Brown replied. "Two masked men held up the Diamond Mart on Sixth Avenue. They got away with a million dollars' worth of jewelry."

"I thought Tim Nolan was arrested," Mrs. Brown said.

"He was questioned, not arrested," Chief

Brown corrected. "I always believed that Nolan and a friend, a man named Daniel Davenport, pulled the holdup. There wasn't any proof, though."

Encyclopedia sat quietly. He knew his mother and father were discussing the case for his benefit.

His father filled in the facts.

Nolan and Davenport had met, Chief Brown said, while both were in prison in South Carolina. They became friendly because of a shared interest—codes. Nolan was let out first. He settled in Idaville and started a small palm-tree nursery. It barely yielded him a living.

Davenport came to live with Nolan a week before the jewelry-store holdup. During the holdup, one gunman's mask slipped. A clerk thought she recognized Nolan. But she wasn't absolutely sure.

"I remember now," Mrs. Brown said. "The clerk refused to testify against him, and no trace of the stolen jewelry ever turned up."

"Davenport hasn't been seen since the holdup," Chief Brown said. "My hunch is that he and Nolan decided to hide the loot until things cooled down."

"Didn't you search Nolan's house, dear?"

"I got a court order this morning," Chief Brown said. "Officers Lewis and Maloney just about took Nolan's place apart. They didn't find one piece of the stolen jewelry."

"Is there some mystery about Nolan's death yesterday?" Mrs. Brown inquired.

"Yes and no," Chief Brown answered. "Nolan suffered from a bad heart for many years. Yesterday morning he had a stroke. He must have realized he was dying. With his last strength, he managed to put his will on the kitchen table. It leaves everything he owns, including his palm-tree nursery, to Davenport."

"What's suspicious about that?" Mrs. Brown asked.

"Nothing about the will itself—just about a sheet from his desk calendar. It was clipped to the will," said Chief Brown.

He took out his pocket notebook and leafed through the pages.

"I copied what Nolan wrote on the sheet," he said. "Here it is."

He handed the notebook to Mrs. Brown.

She read what he had copied. "It has Davenport's name and address," she said, "and four words I don't understand."

She handed the notebook to Encyclopedia.

"What do you make of the four words, Leroy?"

Encyclopedia read the four words below Davenport's name and address: "Nom Utes Sweden Hurts."

Mrs. Brown looked at him hopefully. Usually, he needed to ask only one question to solve a case before dessert. They were still on the soup.

Encyclopedia leaned back and closed his eyes. He always closed his eyes when he did his hardest thinking.

After several seconds, he opened his eyes and asked his question.

"Is there a young fir tree in Mr. Nolan's palm-tree nursery?"

Chief Brown thought a moment. "Yes, there is . . . one. On the south side of the house. How did you know?"

"The four words say so," Encyclopedia answered.

"They do?" said Chief Brown.

"See for yourself," Encyclopedia urged.

Chief Brown studied the four words—
Nom Utes Sweden Hurts. He shook his head
and passed the notebook to Mrs. Brown
again. "Can you figure it out?"

"*Nom* is a shortening of *nominative*, a
grammatical term," stated Mrs. Brown, who
had taught English and other subjects in
high school. "*Utes* are an American Indian
tribe. Sweden is a country in northern
Europe. *Hurts* is 'hurts.'"

She lifted her gaze to Encyclopedia and
shook her head.

"I can't figure it out," she confessed.

"Davenport disappeared right after the
holdup," Encyclopedia reminded her. "As
Dad said, Davenport and Nolan must have
hidden the stolen jewelry. Probably not
more than a week or so ago, Nolan changed
the hiding place."

"You think that he tried to tell Davenport
by phone and failed to reach him?" Mrs.
Brown asked. "So he wrote the four words
as he was dying?"

Chief Brown nodded. "We'll find Davenport now that we know his address."

"He'll learn he has been left the palm-tree nursery," Mrs. Brown said. "And the four words will tell him where the jewelry is hidden!"

"Right," Encyclopedia said. "The code is simple, especially as it's written on a sheet from a calendar. Davenport will understand it easily. Still, it wouldn't make much sense to someone who isn't looking for a hiding place."

"Leroy!" Mrs. Brown exclaimed. "What do the four words mean?"

"You already guessed, Mom. They tell where the jewelry is hidden."

Mrs. Brown looked ready to explode with impatience. *"Where?"*

Encyclopedia smiled.

"Why, under the fifth word," he said.

WHAT WAS THE FIFTH WORD?

(Turn to page 73 for the solution to The Case of the Fifth Word.)

The Case of the Teacup

Encyclopedia helped his father solve mysteries year-round. During the summer, he helped the children of the neighborhood as well.

When school let out, he opened his own detective agency in the family garage. Every morning he hung out his sign:

```
BROWN
DETECTIVE AGENCY
13 Rover Avenue
LEROY BROWN
President
No case too small
25¢ per day plus expenses
```

The first customer Monday morning was Becky Regan. Becky was only nine, but already she was collecting chinaware for her future house.

"What does *etiquette* mean?" she asked.

"Simply put, it means having good manners," Encyclopedia answered.

"I'd rather have my cup," Becky said. "Bugs Meany took it."

"Uh-oh," Encyclopedia murmured. "Bugs, Bugs."

Bugs Meany was the leader of a gang of tough older boys. They called themselves the Tigers. They should have called themselves the Steel Clocks. They were always giving some little kid a hard time.

"Are you sure it was Bugs?" Encyclopedia asked.

"Of course I am," Becky said. "How could I be mistaken? Bugs looks so much like himself."

Encyclopedia needed a second to shake that one off.

Becky said, "I'd just bought the cup at the flea market. Bugs stopped me on my way home and faked me out."

She explained. At first Bugs had laughed and said he'd get her a violin to go with the cup. When Becky told him the cup might be valuable, he stopped laughing.

"Bugs talked me into trading the cup for his crash course in etiquette," Becky said. "He claimed that in a week I'd know how to use forty-three different pieces of silverware."

"When did Bugs learn to count to forty-three?" Encyclopedia said. "Besides, he wouldn't know a fish fork from a lobster dancing."

Becky nodded ruefully. "I've been thinking the same thing."

She laid a quarter on the gas can beside Encyclopedia. "I want to hire you. Get back my cup."

"The first step," Encyclopedia said, "is to go and see Bugs."

"You go," Becky said. "Bugs might get mad and use me for a door knocker. That's too much exercise for a small person like me."

It took some doing, but Encyclopedia got Becky to go along. She had to identify the cup.

The Tigers' clubhouse was an unused toolshed behind Mr. Sweeney's Auto Body Shop. Bugs was alone. On an orange crate next to him was a white cup.

"Th-There it is," Becky said.

Bugs growled, "Make like the Wright brothers and take off."

"Maybe we should let sleeping bugs lie," Becky whispered nervously. "I only paid twenty cents for the cup."

"Stay close," Encyclopedia whispered back. "I've dealt with Bugs before."

To the Tigers' leader he said, "I heard about your course in etiquette."

Bugs sighed. "How rumors do get around! So many people have inquired about the course that I'm thinking of starting one. With us Tigers as teachers, the return of good manners to America would no longer be in doubt."

He picked up the white cup by the handle and daintily curled his little finger.

"I'd teach you how to take tea with the President," he said, glancing at Becky. "You'd be in demand everywhere."

"Spare me the society news," Becky retorted, moving quickly behind Encyclope-

dia. "You fooled me with your phony course in etiquette. Hand over my cup!"

"What cup?" Bugs said.

"The one you're holding," Becky cried.

Bugs's nose went up as if seeking fresh air. "I'm afraid you're quite mistaken, miss. This is *my* cup."

"You're lying!" Becky screamed.

Bugs looked pained. "My dear young lady, you are clearly in need of instruction. Never say, 'You're lying!' Practice etiquette. Be polite."

Before Becky could say anything at all, Encyclopedia stepped in.

"Where did you get the cup, Bugs?" he said.

"From Fu Chee," Bugs replied.

"Who is he?" Becky snapped.

"Fu Chee owned the Chinese restaurant on Fullerton Avenue," Bugs answered.

"The restaurant closed down last year," Encyclopedia said. "It's now a doughnut shop."

"True," Bugs said sadly. "This was Fu Chee's own teacup. He gave it to me when I ate at his restaurant the day before it closed.

I was the only customer ever to finish his shrimp in lobster sauce without taking some home in a doggy bag. He said he'd never forget me."

"Encyclopedia, question Fu Chee," Becky urged.

"You better have the plane fare," Bugs warned. "He moved to Utah."

Becky kicked the ground. "With Fu Chee gone, I can't prove I'm telling the truth," she whispered to Encyclopedia. "Darn it! Bugs outsmarted us."

"Bugs outsmarted himself," Encyclopedia corrected. "Fu Chee didn't give him the cup."

HOW DID ENCYCLOPEDIA KNOW?

*(Turn to page 75 for the solution to
The Case of the Teacup.)*

The Case of the Broken Vase

Bugs Meany had one goal in life. It was to get even with Encyclopedia Brown.

Bugs hated being outsmarted all the time. He dreamed of pounding Encyclopedia like a fence post, after which the detective could wear his socks as earmuffs.

Bugs never used muscle, however. Whenever he was tempted, he remembered Sally Kimball, Encyclopedia's junior partner in the detective agency.

Not only was Sally the prettiest girl in fifth

grade, she could do what no kid thought possible—blister Bugs's bluster.

Whenever they fought, Bugs ended up on his back, panting like a hot chicken.

"Bugs claims you always hit him first, when he isn't looking," Encyclopedia said with a grin. "You never give him a chance to warm up his fighting blood."

"He doesn't need to warm up," Sally replied. "He's got permanent sunstroke."

"Bugs hates you as much as he hates me," warned Encyclopedia. "He'll get even any way he can. You know his favorite saying."

" 'If at first you don't succeed, try something sneaky,' " Sally said. She jabbed the air—*pow, pow, pow.* "Let him try, the big ape!"

Her eyes widened. Bugs Meany had stepped into the Brown Detective Agency.

"Why not bury the hatchet?" he purred.

He laid a dollar bill beside Encyclopedia and didn't ask for change.

"Be at my house tonight at eight o'clock sharp," he said. "I'll leave the front door unlocked and the lights off so you won't be seen. Wait for me in the living room."

The detectives were speechless.

Bugs glanced around quickly.

"Don't breathe a word of this to anyone," he cautioned. "It's top secret. The safety of Idaville may depend on you."

Encyclopedia started to say no thanks. But Sally was already on her feet.

"We'll take the case," she agreed.

"How come?" Encyclopedia asked after Bugs had left.

"Bugs is up to something, and I want to know what," Sally declared.

Encyclopedia was still uneasy at eight o'clock. Bugs's house was silent and dark.

The detectives slipped through the front door and turned into the living room. The shades were drawn. Encyclopedia could see less than a yard ahead of him.

Suddenly, things happened.

First, a crash sounded in the living room near Encyclopedia. Then footsteps thumped on the stairs.

The lights flashed on. Officer Friedman stood in the doorway with his hand on the switch.

"Bugs, are you okay?" he called.

Bugs groaned. He was lying facedown among pieces of a broken yellow vase. The pieces were scattered over the floor from his head to his feet.

The neck of the vase, wrapped in a rag, lay on his right. Near it was a hard hat.

Bugs staggered up, holding the back of his head. "There are your burglars!" he cried. "Read 'em their rights!"

"Make sense, Bugs," Encyclopedia demanded.

"Bugs told me his house has been robbed twice in the past month," Officer Friedman said. "The robbers took stuff children might steal."

"Yesterday I heard these two talking in the Brown garage," Bugs said. "Ms. Muscles was saying, 'His folks are out of town, and Bugs stays at the Tigers' clubhouse until nine. We can clean out the place in an hour.' "

"When Bugs told me what he had overheard," Officer Friedman said, "I decided to hide upstairs."

"Bugs hired us to come here!" Sally protested.

"One of them must have sneaked up behind me and hit me on the back of the head with the vase," Bugs said. "Thank heaven my hard hat cushioned the blow."

"Do you often wear a hat indoors?" Officer Friedman inquired.

"It's my thinking hat," Bugs said. "I wear it at night, when I think my hardest."

Sally exploded. "What can you think about besides a bagel? Your brain is made of cream cheese."

Bugs put his hands in his pockets as if searching for a reply.

His eyes lit up. "I was figuring out why a stomach doesn't digest itself. When I come up with the reason, the President will probably name a park after me."

"If anything is named after you," Sally retorted, "it will be a waste site."

She turned to Officer Friedman. "Dust the vase for fingerprints."

The policeman shook his head. "There won't be fingerprints. That's why the rag is wrapped around the neck of the vase. It's where it was held."

"Can't you see Bugs is trying to frame us?" Sally exclaimed.

"I fear this poor girl is past medical help," Bugs sighed. "Find her a warm and comfortable cell."

Officer Friedman frowned. "I don't know who's telling the truth. We'll have to straighten everything out at headquarters."

All at once Sally looked worried. "Encyclopedia, say something. Don't let Bugs get away with this!"

"He won't," Encyclopedia assured her.

WHY NOT?

(*Turn to page 77 for the solution to The Case of the Broken Vase.*)

The Case of the Three Vans

Chief Brown hung up the kitchen telephone.

"I've got to leave," he said. "It seems we have another case with a message in code. This time it's a kidnapping."

"Why don't you take Leroy along?" Mrs. Brown suggested. "He's so good at codes."

Encyclopedia stopped scraping the dinner plates. He held his breath until his father smiled.

"Let's go, Leroy," Chief Brown said.

Encyclopedia let out a whoop. Being with

his father on a real police case was the thrill of thrills.

He whipped through the last two dishes and was seated in the patrol car before his father even got behind the wheel.

As they drove, Chief Brown told Encyclopedia what little he knew about the case.

"A man named Harry Dunn was kidnapped this morning," he said. "About an hour ago, the kidnappers telephoned his sister, Mrs. Allen. They demanded half a million dollars in ransom."

"What about the coded message, Dad?"

"We'll know more when we see it."

As they pulled up to Harry Dunn's big house, Officer Kent greeted them at the curb.

He said, "Harry Dunn's sister, Mrs. Allen, is in the living room. Also a neighbor, Mr. Tradd. He may have seen Harry Dunn being kidnapped."

Mrs. Allen was a pale, middle-aged woman. Her eyes were red from crying. Chief Brown questioned her first.

"I received a telephone call late this afternoon from a man with a deep voice," she said, sobbing. "He said my brother had been kidnapped and the ransom was half a million dollars. I'd be told where to leave the money later."

"You called the police right away?" asked Chief Brown.

"No, first I called Harry," Mrs. Allen said. "There was no answer. So I drove here and let myself in—I have a key. The house was empty. That's when I called the police."

Chief Brown turned to the neighbor, Mr. Tradd. "What can you tell us, sir?"

"About ten o'clock this morning, I borrowed some garden tools from Harry," Mr. Tradd said. "He didn't answer the doorbell when I returned the tools at noon. The garage door was open, so I left the tools on his workbench."

"Which house is yours?" Chief Brown inquired.

"The one right across the street," Mr. Tradd replied. "I was planting in the front yard. So I saw everyone who came to Harry's front door."

"The back door was locked from the inside," Mrs. Allen put in. "Whoever kid-

napped Harry used the front door."

"Did you see anyone at the front door?" Chief Brown asked Mr. Tradd.

"While I was planting, three delivery vans drove up, about fifteen or twenty minutes apart. But each of them blocked my view of the front door," Mr. Tradd said.

"So Mr. Dunn could have been taken out the door and placed in one of the vans," Chief Brown said, "without your seeing him."

"That's possible," Mr. Tradd agreed.

Chief Brown took out his pocket notebook. "Can you describe the three vans?"

"Each van had its company's name painted on the side—Bill's Fish Market, ABC TV Repair, and Sun Drug Store."

"Was that the order in which they parked at Mr. Dunn's front door?" Chief Brown asked.

"I just don't remember," Mr. Tradd answered. "I really didn't think the vans were important. I didn't know about the kidnapping."

Officer Kent said, "I checked the companies. All the deliveries were scheduled."

He handed Chief Brown a small sheet of paper.

"This is the note I found on a pad by the telephone in the family room," he said.

Chief Brown studied the note. He gave up and passed it to Encyclopedia.

"What do you make of it, Leroy?"

The boy detective read:

Study Outbursts Defending Hiccoughing

Crabcake

Chief Brown showed the note to Mrs. Allen. "Is this your brother's handwriting?"

Mrs. Allen put on her eyeglasses. "Yes . . . it looks like his."

"Did your brother like to write coded messages?" Chief Brown said.

"As a boy he did," Mrs. Allen answered. "He still enjoys word puzzles." She dried her eyes. "I kept telling him not to live in this big house all alone!"

Encyclopedia was thinking hard. He had closed his eyes. He opened them and asked his one question.

"Is Crabcake Mr. Dunn's nickname?"

"I never heard him called that," Mrs. Allen replied. She blew her nose.

"It's the newspaper's fault," she said bitterly. "It printed our pictures when Harry and I each inherited a million dollars last month. That gave somebody ideas!"

She began to weep again.

Chief Brown took Encyclopedia aside.

"Maybe the vans and the crazy note have nothing to do with the kidnapping, Leroy," he remarked.

"No, Dad," said Encyclopedia. "The word *Crabcake* tells which van took Mr. Dunn away. The top four words give the key to the code."

WHICH ONE?

*(Turn to page 79 for the solution to
The Case of the Three Vans.)*

The Case of
the Rented Canoes

Clouds hid the sun Saturday morning. Nevertheless, Encyclopedia and his pal Tommy Barkdull decided to go ahead and rent a canoe.

They nearly changed their minds at Captain Pete's.

The old sailor's freshly painted canoes were neatly tied to the little dock by their front ends. They were not just in the water. They were partly under it.

Half an inch of rainwater lay in the bottoms.

"Sorry, you'll get wet feet," Captain Pete apologized. "I painted the canoes the other day. As I launched the last one, I twisted my ankle and had to go home. The canoes stayed out in the rain, but there's not enough water in them to matter."

"The water won't bother us," Tommy said.

Captain Pete rang up the rental fee and laid two paddles and two life jackets on the counter.

"You've been here before," he said. "You know the rules."

Tommy nodded. "Don't run the canoe ashore unless the beach is soft, without rocks."

"If we see lightning, come in fast," Encyclopedia said.

Captain Pete grinned. "Enjoy yourselves."

The boys chose canoe number six. Since they were both the same weight, it didn't matter who sat in the back and steered.

"It's your turn," Tommy said. "I steered last time."

Encyclopedia wasn't about to protest. Being able to paddle and steer was more fun than sitting in front and just paddling.

He sloshed through the rainwater in the bottom of the canoe and took his seat in the back. Tommy got in and cast off.

They stroked across the Idaville River and entered the tree-lined waterways of the state park.

After a while they came to the park ranger's station. It stood on a rocky little island, a patch of solid ground surrounded by mangrove trees.

The door was wide open. The patrol boat that normally was tied to the dock in front was gone.

The boys were about to investigate when they saw black storm clouds moving toward them.

"Let's make waves!" Tommy yelped.

They paddled back to Captain Pete's as fast as they could.

Captain Pete was waiting for them.

He had the boys haul the canoe onto land. The previous night's rainwater spilled out as they turned it over on its rack.

Carefully, Captain Pete examined the freshly painted pink-and-orange bottom.

"Not a scratch on her," he muttered.

"What's this all about?" Encyclopedia asked.

"Just making sure," Captain Pete said. "Three fishing rods were stolen from the ranger's station."

Earlier in the morning, he explained, the ranger had overheard a boater's distress call on the radio. He had dashed off in his powerboat. He must not have closed the door securely, and the wind blew it open.

As he pulled away, he glimpsed a pink-and-orange canoe approaching the station.

"It had to be one of my canoes," Captain Pete said. "I purposely use colors no one else uses."

"Who was in the canoe?" Tommy asked.

"The ranger didn't notice," Captain Pete replied. "He was too concerned with the distress call. When he came back to the station an hour later, the three fishing rods were missing."

"Who else rented a canoe this morning?" asked Encyclopedia.

"The Baldwin sisters went out half an hour before you," Captain Pete said. "And the Smith twins left right after them."

"Here they come," said Tommy, motioning toward two pink-and-orange canoes on the river.

First to tie up were the Smith twins, Barry and Gary. They were powerful, one-hundred-sixty-pound high-school wrestlers.

The Baldwin sisters came in shortly afterward. Peggy, a small sixth-grader, sat in front. Nancy, a big eighth-grader, sat in back.

They tied the front of the canoe to the dock, as the twins had done.

The twins and the sisters claimed they knew nothing about the stolen fishing rods.

"We never even got out of our canoe," Gary insisted.

"Nor did we," Nancy said.

Their canoes had neither fishing rods on the inside nor scratches on the outside.

"Heck," Tommy whispered. "Whoever stole the rods had time to hide them among the trees. Why did Captain Pete look for scratches?"

"He probably figured the thieves beached their canoe on the rocks behind the ranger's station, where there is less chance of being seen," Encyclopedia said. "Scratches would tell which canoe it was."

"They could have used the ranger's dock," Tommy pointed out. "Come to think of it, so could any boater. Maybe the fishing rods were stolen by someone else."

"No," Encyclopedia said.

"How can you be so sure?" Tommy inquired.

"When we brought the canoes in," Encyclopedia replied, "we all made wet sneaker prints on Captain Pete's dock—you, me, the twins, and the sisters."

"Of course we did," Tommy said. "All three canoes still had rainwater in them."

"True," Encyclopedia said. "But there was one set of footprints too many, and they belong to the thief."

WHO WAS THE THIEF?

(*Turn to page 81 for the solution to The Case of the Rented Canoes.*)

The Case of the Brain Game

Tyrone Taylor was a friendly boy who was known throughout the neighborhood as Romeo Glue.

He was always stuck on some girl.

"Who is she this month?" Encyclopedia asked Sally as they biked to Tyrone's birthday party.

"Cindy Hayes, the blonde in Mrs. Benson's fifth-grade class," Sally said. "She looks as if she'd lose her way walking upstairs. But she's smart. She's doing seventh-grade math."

Cindy Hayes was also quick on her feet. She won the first game at the party, musical chairs played blindfolded.

"The music was wrong," Sally complained, rubbing her leg. "It should have been 'Lullaby to Shin Splints.' "

For the second contest, pie eating, there were only four contestants. Chester Jenkins, Encyclopedia's widest pal, scared off everyone else. As soon as the eating began, Chester showed why he was nicknamed Jet Jaws. He won by half a pie.

"You only go around once in life," Chester told the detectives. "You've got to eat all the banana-cream pies you can."

After he waddled off, Sally said, "Chester is sure to win another prize, first one in the dining room."

Encyclopedia defended his pal. "Chester is more than an appetite in shoes. Don't forget that he won the brain game last year."

"That's because Tyrone didn't let you play," Sally replied.

Encyclopedia had not been allowed to enter any brain games since Tyrone's fifth birthday party. "You're too smart," Tyrone had said then, and every year since.

"Tyrone is sweet, but unfair," Sally muttered.

"It's his party," Encyclopedia said. "Maybe today I'll win something. I came close two years ago."

Two years ago he had placed second in a new game, Make Like. The idea then was to make like a walrus singing "The Yellow Rose of Texas."

Encyclopedia had done well, tying with Linda Mills. After a sing-off, Linda had been awarded the prize.

"You were gypped in the sing-off," Sally said. "Linda sounded like a moose stuck in the mud. At every one of his parties, Tyrone makes sure his girl of the month wins a prize."

"Today will be different," Encyclopedia said.

"Why?"

"Tyrone's mother will do the judging—at least of the brain game."

"I'll believe it when I see it," Sally grumbled.

She didn't grumble for long. The next

game was shooting baskets. She sank six shots in a row and won easily.

The games went on for another hour.

Farnsworth Grant won at darts. Benny Breslin won the croquet tournament. Edith Martin won Simon Says. There were prizes for all the winners.

Adorabelle Walsh won the cherry spit for distance. Encyclopedia had his best finish. He breathed in when he should have breathed out. He wound up coughing and nearly choking. The war in his throat shot out the third longest spit.

Shortly before three o'clock, Mrs. Taylor, Tyrone's mother, announced the brain game.

The children went inside. Chester Jenkins took a position close to the dining room. Encyclopedia settled on a chair in the rear.

Mrs. Taylor passed out pencils and paper.

"The object is to write down nine common body parts that have only three letters," she said. "First, put your name at the top of the sheet."

She waited for the children to write their names.

"When you have written nine body parts, raise your hand," she said. "Ready, everyone? You have ten minutes. Go!"

Encyclopedia watched Cindy Hayes, Tyrone's latest girlfriend. She wrote for six or seven minutes. Then she stopped. Her brow wrinkled.

None of the other children wrote anything for the last three minutes.

"They're stumped," thought Encyclopedia.

"Time's up!" Mrs. Taylor called. "Has anyone got nine?"

Heads shook glumly.

"How many have eight?"

Chester and Cindy raised their hands.

Mrs. Taylor took their papers and read them. Tyrone looked over her shoulder.

"We have a tie," she said. "I'll give Chester and Cindy three more minutes to think of a body part they missed."

She handed Chester and Cindy their papers.

"Ready, start!"

Tyrone left the room and came back a minute later, chewing.

Cindy glanced at him questioningly.

Tyrone stopped chewing and grinned. Then he blew a small pink bubble and quickly sucked it back into his mouth.

Cindy wrote on her paper. "Nine! I have nine!" she called.

Mrs. Taylor took her list and read it. "Nine it is."

She gave Cindy her prize, a checkers set.

Sally cornered Encyclopedia. "Cindy cheated, but I don't know how. I just know it! Encyclopedia, prove Tyrone helped her!"

"I'll have to see her list," Encyclopedia said. "But I'm pretty sure I know how Tyrone helped."

HOW?

*(Turn to page 83 for the solution to
The Case of the Brain Game.)*

The Case of Black Jack's Treasure

Encyclopedia and Sally were biking past the golf course when they spied Otis Dibbs. Otis had on pants.

The detectives stopped and stared.

During the summer, Otis went around the golf course in a bathing suit and snorkel. He recovered golf balls from the ponds and streams. He sold the balls to players who wanted cheap ones to lose again.

"What's wrong, Otis?" Sally called.

"Not a thing," Otis assured her. "Fact is, I'm retiring. It's good-bye to muddy water,

broken bottles, snakes, and snapping tur-
tles. Easy life, here I come!"

"Did somebody leave you a lot of money?"
Encyclopedia inquired.

"Nope," Otis replied. "But soon I'm going
to be independently wealthy. Wilford Wiggins has called a secret meeting for five
o'clock by the sixteenth hole. He promised
to make us little kids crazy rich. We'll be able
to buy our own candy store and give it away
when the candy runs out."

"Oh, not Wilford again," Encyclopedia
said painfully.

Wilford Wiggins was a high-school drop-
out, and too lazy to stretch. He spent his
mornings in bed dreaming up ways to gyp
the children of the neighborhood out of
their savings.

Encyclopedia had always been able to stop
Wilford's phony deals.

Only last week the detective had kept Wilford from selling shares in a pink pill that
was supposed to cure athlete's foot and help
you see in the dark.

"How is Wilford going to make you rich
today?" Sally asked. "With a baseball that
throws itself?"

"He didn't say," Otis answered. "He just promised to put us close to a good thing."

"But not close enough to touch," Encyclopedia said.

"Wilford may be telling the truth this time," Otis protested.

"When has Wilford told the truth?" Sally demanded. "He hates liars so much, he never speaks to himself."

Otis suddenly looked worried. He took a quarter from his pocket. "I'd better hire you to make sure I'm not cheated."

"We'll do our best," Encyclopedia said.

"It's nearly five o'clock," Sally noted. "We'd better move."

Otis led the two detectives to a small, worthless-looking strip of woods past the sixteenth hole.

Wilford Wiggins stood beside a huge old tree. A crowd of boys and girls waited for his words of wealth.

Wilford raised his arms. "Move in closer, everyone!" he shouted. "I don't want any of my young friends to miss this once-in-a-lifetime chance—"

He broke off. He had seen Encyclopedia and Sally with Otis.

He recovered quickly and said, "Every kid is welcome, even nosy-bodies who weren't invited to this secret meeting."

He pulled a sheet of paper from a sack at his feet and held it above his head.

"Do you know what this is?" he cried. "It tells where Black Jack Lefever buried his *treasure!*"

Everyone had heard of Black Jack Lefever, the pirate. He had buried a fortune in Idaville ten feet from a landmark, a small young tree. He had carved his name on the trunk.

"This is a copy of a page from his ship's log," Wilford said. "It gives directions on how to get from the small tree to the buried treasure."

"So what?" hollered Otis. "You can buy a framed copy of that page in every gift store in Idaville. Then all you have to do is find the tree with Black Jack's name on it."

"Right, friend," Wilford said. "Nobody found the tree—till yours truly! *It's this one!*"

He tapped the huge tree beside him.

"With Black Jack's directions and this tree, we can find the place where the treasure is buried!" he sang.

"What are we waiting for?" Otis shouted. "Let's dig!"

"I don't own this land," Wilford pointed out. "We'd have to give back anything we find here today. But we can own the land if each of you buys a share in the treasure. I'm asking a mere five dollars a share. The more shares you buy, the more treasure you'll get."

"First show us Black Jack's name on the tree," Otis hollered.

"It's up there," Wilford said. "According to his notes in the ship's log, Black Jack carved it when the tree was only about eight feet high—more than a century ago. The tree has grown so tall, it's hard to see the carving from the ground."

Wilford took a pair of binoculars from the sack. He handed them to Otis. "Look for yourself."

Otis peered through the binoculars. He raised them slowly up the trunk of the tree, till they were pointed at a spot some twenty feet above the ground.

"I can read something," he gasped. "It's— *Black Jack Lefever!*"

The binoculars were eagerly passed

around. Each child saw the name carved on the tree trunk. Yelps of glee were followed by yelps of greed.

"Remember, don't tell anyone," Wilford warned. "If our secret gets out, the price of this land will soar. We won't be able to afford it. The big shots at the golf club will keep it and get all Black Jack's gold and jewels."

The children swore themselves to secrecy. They lined up to buy shares in the treasure.

"Hold on to your money," Encyclopedia told them. "Black Jack didn't bury his treasure here."

WHAT MADE ENCYCLOPEDIA CERTAIN?

(Turn to page 85 for the solution to The Case of Black Jack's Treasure.)

The Case of the Missing Shopping Bag

Sunday at one o'clock, Encyclopedia biked to Ike Ryan's house for an afternoon of chess.

Ike had just made the first move when his mother entered the room. She was carrying three skirts.

"Fashion show," she announced.

The boys stopped playing. Mr. Ryan, who was seated in an easy chair, laid his newspaper on his lap.

"Let's see what you bought, dear," he said.

Mrs. Ryan held the three skirts, one after

another, to her waist. "Like them?"

"The tan and the plaid are lovely," Mr. Ryan said. "I don't care for the gray one."

"You're right. I don't like it so much as the other two, either," Mrs. Ryan said. "I'll take it back."

She folded the skirts and carried them into the kitchen. Presently Encyclopedia heard her talking on the telephone.

"This is Mrs. Ryan. . . . Yes. . . . Good. . . . In half an hour? . . . Yes, I've decided to get rid of the gray. I don't like it. . . . No, the length is all right."

She returned to the living room.

"I'm off to the shopping center and then to Grandma's," she said. "See you around six."

After she left, the two boys settled down to their chess match. Ike lost three straight games. He threw up his hands.

"Someday I'm going to beat you," he swore.

"How about another?" Encyclopedia suggested. "It's only two-thirty."

"No, thanks," replied Ike. "Yesterday I borrowed a pamphlet on chess from Hewitt

Dawkins. I don't want to be late returning it."

"Good thinking," Encyclopedia said.

Hewitt was seventeen and the biggest chess player in Idaville. He was known for his quick moves and his quicker temper.

Ike said, "Hewitt said that if I didn't return the pamphlet by four o'clock today—oooh, boy. People will start asking me if I've ever been dead."

"Holy cow," Encyclopedia exclaimed. "Get going!"

Ike hurried to the front door. Moments later, he came back holding a white-paper shopping bag. His mouth was open wide, as if he'd just bitten into a mothball.

"Mom took my shopping bag with Hewitt's pamphlet in it!" he wailed.

He explained. He had put the pamphlet into a white-paper shopping bag. Then he had stood the bag by the front door to remind him to return the pamphlet.

"Mom must have put her gray skirt into my shopping bag by mistake," he said. "She left her empty bag behind."

Mr. Ryan lowered his newspaper. "Didn't

you hear her on the telephone? She's gone to return it."

"Where?" Ike blurted.

Encyclopedia pointed to the shopping bag. On it was printed the name Just Skirts, a phone number, and an address.

"The pamphlet has to be at Just Skirts in the Suniland shopping center!" Ike exclaimed. "I'm saved!"

He rushed into the kitchen to call Just Skirts. Encyclopedia heard him dial, hang up, dial, then hang up again.

"Nobody answers," Ike said mournfully.

"I'd drive you," Mr. Ryan said, "but I'm waiting for Harry Clark. We have business to discuss."

He reached into his pocket.

"The number-nine bus stops at the Suniland shopping center," he said. "It's only a ten-minute ride."

He handed the boys bus fare and went back to his newspaper.

Encyclopedia tried to comfort Ike. "You've got more than an hour before you have to return the pamphlet," he said encouragingly.

"Th-That's all?" Ike gurgled. "Do you think Hewitt would really hit an unarmed little kid?"

The Suniland shopping center was a strip of five stores along Gelula Avenue. Just Skirts was at the southern end. A sign, CLOSED FOR INVENTORY, hung in the window.

Ike put his forehead to the glass pane. "There's no one inside. They've quit for the day!"

Encyclopedia was puzzled. "Over the telephone your mother sounded as if she were coming here to bring back the gray skirt."

"I thought so, too," Ike said.

"Maybe she changed her mind and went straight to your grandmother's."

Ike whooped. "So she took the shopping bag with her! Encyclopedia, your brain never stops!"

Ike used a pay phone to call his grandmother.

Encyclopedia sat down on an iron bench. Something was bothering him. He looked at the store signs hanging below the ceiling of the covered walk.

Next to Just Skirts was a hardware store.

Then came a beauty parlor, a drugstore, and a dry cleaner.

The detective closed his eyes and did some deep thinking. It took half a minute to come up with the answer.

He opened his eyes and saw Ike standing by the telephone, clutching his wrist.

"What are you doing?" Encyclopedia asked.

"I'm taking my pulse," Ike whimpered. "There's no answer at Grandma's. Mom must have driven her somewhere." He let out a groan. "What can Hewitt do to me that will make people ask if I was ever dead?"

Encyclopedia could name a dozen things. He said merely, "Cheer up. I know where your mother is."

WHERE?

*(Turn to page 87 for the solution to
The Case of the Missing Shopping Bag.)*

The Case of the Disgusting Sneakers

On the day of the Disgusting Sneaker Contest, Phoebe Eastwood, last year's champion, walked into the Brown Detective Agency. She had on shoes.

Encyclopedia immediately knew something was afoot.

All year Phoebe had prepared for the defense of her title by wearing the same pair of sneakers. She had them in really disgusting shape.

"I want to hire you," she said, laying twenty-five cents on the gas can beside Encyclopedia. "Some girl swiped my right sneaker."

Bad as her left sneaker was, her right sneaker was worse. It had two large holes in front. Her toes poked through like stunned tadpoles.

"I kept the sneakers outside the garage," Phoebe said. "Mom never allows them in the house. She says the smell would make an elephant faint."

All at once Encyclopedia wished he were somewhere else, like somersaulting down a ski jump.

"Go on," he said bravely.

"An hour ago I was sitting in the garage, clipping my toenails, the ones that show through the right sneaker," Phoebe said. "The door was open, and I noticed a girl running across my yard."

"Who was it?" Sally asked.

"I only saw her back," Phoebe said. "But she was carrying my sneaker."

"Whoever stole your sneaker wants to stop you from winning again," Sally said. "That means she's in the Disgusting Sneaker Contest herself."

"Then go out to South Park and watch the contest," Phoebe urged. "Maybe you can spot the thief."

Encyclopedia cared less than zero about getting up close and personal with the rottenest sneakers in Idaville.

Still . . . duty called.

As they biked to South Park, Phoebe told the detectives all about the Disgusting Sneaker Contest.

The event raised money for charity through entrance fees and sponsors. There were only two rules. Sneakers had to belong to the child whose feet were in them, and damage couldn't be caused by anything but natural wear.

"The judges grade sneakers on a scale of one to twenty," Phoebe said. "They look at eyelets, tongues, soles, heels, and overall condition."

The judging had begun when they reached South Park. Ann Little, Phoebe's classmate, hurried over to her.

"I was getting worried," Ann said. "I thought something happened to you."

"Something did," Phoebe replied sadly.

"Somebody stole my right sneaker while I was clipping my nails."

"I don't see Bugs Meany," Sally remarked, glancing around. "He's been bragging all week that he's a 'shoe-in.'"

"Bugs was thrown out on his ear," Ann answered happily. "He beat up his sneakers with an electric weed cutter, but he didn't fool the judges."

"Have you been judged?" Phoebe asked.

"At the moment I'm in the lead," Ann said. "But Stinky Redmond, Tessie Bottoms, and lots of others haven't had their turn."

"Tessie's just been called," Sally said.

Tessie, an eighth-grader, strutted up confidently. She removed both sneakers and laid them on the table in front of the judges.

All the judges wore rubber gloves for protection. They picked up each sneaker and examined it at arm's length.

Tessie received seventeen points, putting her in the lead. She paraded over to Phoebe.

"Top that, kiddo!" she gloated.

"Knock it off, Tessie," Ann said. "Phoebe's not in the contest this year. Somebody stole her right sneaker while she was clipping her toenails."

"If she ever learns what socks are for, she won't have to worry about her toenails," Tessie jeered.

Suddenly there was a big fuss by the table. Mrs. Carstairs, one of the judges, had swooned and couldn't continue.

"You've got to smell this contest to believe it," she muttered as she was helped away. "I should have brought a gas mask."

"Maybe the judges should get prizes," Sally observed.

Encyclopedia mumbled. His mind was on something else.

Something he had heard or seen bothered him. He was trying to remember what it was when Stinky Redmond's name was called.

"Stinky could have dressed up as a girl and stolen Phoebe's sneaker," Sally said. "He's tricky enough to slip a full moon past a werewolf."

Stinky wore black-and-white jogging sneakers. He laid them on the judges' table and looked cockily at Tessie.

"Did you see that?" Phoebe exclaimed. "He looked at Tessie as if she were his biggest rival, not me. He knows I can't defeat

him because I have only one sneaker!"

"Phoebe's right," Ann said. "Stinky gave himself away. He's the thief!"

"Someone ought to wrinkle his chin," Sally said.

"Wait," Encyclopedia cautioned. He was still trying to remember.

The winners were announced at three o'clock. Stinky won. Tessie finished second.

Sally and Phoebe and Ann cheered an instant later. Ann had taken third.

Encyclopedia didn't groan or cheer. He had remembered.

"You're the thief," he said to . . .

WHO WAS THE THIEF?

(*Turn to page 89 for the solution to The Case of the Disgusting Sneakers.*)

The Case of
the Smugglers'
Secret

On Friday, Encyclopedia and Charlie Stuart went camping. They pitched their pup tent by a stream miles from town.

The next morning they were awakened at dawn by the tapping of rain—and by the noise of a helicopter flying too low.

"Sounds like it's going to crash!" Charlie yelped.

Both boys struggled out of their sleeping bags and into their clothes.

They raced from their campsite, across a bridge and into a thick wood.

The helicopter had not crashed. It had

landed in a muddy clearing.

"Something's funny," Encyclopedia whispered. "Get behind a tree and stay down."

A gray van drove up. The driver got out. He and the pilot moved three large boxes from the helicopter to the van.

"Smugglers," Charlie breathed.

The men shook hands, and the pilot got back inside the helicopter. It took off in a whir of blades. The van rocked but did not move. A rear wheel whined, spinning in the mud.

The driver got out of the van and swore, looked at the wheel, then swore again. He started for the wood.

"He's seen us!" Charlie squeaked.

"He's coming for branches to put under the tire," Encyclopedia said. "However . . . let's get out of here!"

"I don't know how you do it," Charlie said. "That's exactly what I was thinking."

The boys hightailed it back to their tent.

"I've got to get to a telephone and call Dad," Encyclopedia panted, climbing on his bike.

"Something tells me I'm going with you," Charlie said shakily.

The rain was falling harder as they

reached the outskirts of Idaville.

None of the stores were open, but on Third Street they saw a pay phone. It didn't do them any good. They had only fifteen cents between them.

"I'll bike on home," Encyclopedia said.

"You'll be too late," Charlie replied. "By the time your dad gets to the clearing, the rain will have washed away all trace of the helicopter and the van. He won't—"

Charlie's jaw dropped in surprise. The gray van was coming down the street.

"Let's follow it," Encyclopedia said.

"I wish us a lot of very good luck," Charlie said with a moan.

The van turned left into an alley and stopped at the rear entrance to R. C. Duggan's Import-Export Shop.

The driver and a big, dark-haired man unloaded the boxes. Encyclopedia and Charlie hid behind a dumpster.

"That does it," the big man said. "Ditch the van and get back here."

The van roared off. The big man went into the shop, leaving the door open a crack.

"Let's take a peek," Encyclopedia said.

"Not me," Charlie replied. "It's better to be a coward for a day than a dead fifth-grader for the rest of my life."

"Just a quick look around," Encyclopedia said. "In and out before the driver returns."

"Okay," Charlie murmured. He gulped and pressed his hand to his chest. "Be still, my foolish heart."

The boys slipped through the door and entered a storeroom. Encyclopedia heard the big man moving in a front room.

The three large boxes stood against the storeroom wall.

In the dim light of the room's two naked bulbs, Encyclopedia read the writing on each box.

Remite: Tienda de Antigüedades
113 Mindello
Lima, Perú

> *Señor Hernández*
> *Tienda de Antigüedades*
> *771 Salzedo*
> *Barcelona, España*

"What does this mean?" Charlie whispered.

"It's Spanish," Encyclopedia replied. "It says the three boxes were shipped from Peru, a country in South America, and are going to a man in Spain."

He pulled the tape off one box and opened it. Inside were clay pots. They appeared very old and were wrapped in foam material to keep them from breaking.

"Look in them," Charlie urged.

Encyclopedia looked. The pots were empty.

"I figured we'd find something valuable hidden inside," Charlie muttered. "Like diamonds."

"They seem to be copies of ancient Indian pots," Encyclopedia Brown said thoughtfully. "South American Indians made pottery more than three thousand years ago. If these pots were real, they'd be worth a fortune."

He pointed to the word *copy*, painted in white on the bottom of each pot. The paint rubbed off.

"Let's open the other two boxes," Charlie said. "There has to be *something* more."

There was—more old-looking pots. Each

had the word *copy* painted on its bottom.

"I get it!" Charlie said. "Somebody is smuggling fake old pots. When they reach Spain, the word *copy* will be wiped off. The buyer will be told the pots are three thousand years old!"

Encyclopedia did not answer. He was puzzled.

If Charlie was right, what was the point of all the secrecy?

The boys sealed up the boxes and sneaked outside. As they pedaled away, Encyclopedia suddenly understood.

"Of course!" he exclaimed. "They're smuggling . . ."

WHAT?

*(Turn to page 91 for the solution to
The Case of the Smugglers' Secret.)*

Solution to
The Case of the Fifth Word

To tell Davenport where he'd hidden the stolen jewelry, Nolan wrote a four-word code.

As the key to the code, he wrote the four words on a sheet from a desk calendar.

The four words stood for days of the week.

Nolan dropped the letters *d-a-y*. Then he used the other letters to form words.

So, *Nom* = Monday, *Utes* = Tuesday, *Sweden* = Wednesday, and *Hurts* = Thursday.

The unwritten fifth word was *Fir,* or Friday.

The jewelry was found inside a twenty-gallon jug of earth from which grew the young fir tree in Nolan's nursery—just as Encyclopedia had foreseen.

Solution to
The Case of the Teacup

Bugs claimed the teacup belonged to Fu Chee himself.

He felt safe in telling the lie. He knew Encyclopedia could not check his story. The restaurant was no more, and Fu Chee had moved to Utah.

It was his word, Bugs thought, against Becky's.

But Encyclopedia spotted something that

Bugs had overlooked.

The handle on the white cup.

Bugs had "picked up the white cup by the handle," remember?

Chinese teacups do not have handles.

Caught in his own lie, Bugs returned the cup to Becky.

Solution to
The Case of the Broken Vase

Bugs lied about overhearing Encyclopedia and Sally planning to rob his house.

He also lied about his house being robbed twice in the past month. He wanted Encyclopedia and Sally to look like housebreakers.

But Bugs made a mistake. He said someone had sneaked up behind him and hit him on the back of the head.

If that was true, Encyclopedia realized, Bugs wouldn't have fallen onto the pieces.

He would have fallen forward, all right. But the pieces of the vase, or almost all of them, would have dropped behind him and not in front of him.

All the pieces were between "his head and feet."

Solution to
The Case of the Three Vans

After his rescue by the police, Mr. Dunn told what had happened.

The man who brought his TV set from the repair shop had bent to plug it in. As he did, Mr. Dunn saw his back pocket. It held a gun.

Alarmed, Mr. Dunn left a note in code in case there was trouble. The deliveryman, who turned out to be the kidnapper, read the note and asked what it meant.

Mr. Dunn told him it was just a reminder to himself to have his sister, a nurse, read up on his hiccoughing. He said Crabcake was her pet name for him.

Encyclopedia saw that the top four words gave the code away. Each word had three letters in alphabetical order.

The key word, *Crabcake*, was underlined. The letters were *a-b-c*.

Thus, *ABC TV Repair!*

Solution to
The Case of the Rented Canoes

In the twins' canoe, the water lay evenly because they were about the same weight, as were Encyclopedia and Tommy.

Not so with the Baldwin sisters. Nancy, the heavier, sat in back. Since the canoes were tied to the dock by the front end, she got in first and out last.

So when Peggy got in, the rainwater had pooled at Nancy's end. Peggy's sneakers might have got damp, but they should have dried by the time she got out.

Yet Peggy had left "wet footprints" on the dock.

Because of Encyclopedia's eagle eye, the sisters confessed.

Seeing the door of the ranger station open and the ranger's boat gone, Peggy had waded ashore behind the station to investigate. She wore her sneakers because of the rocks. Spotting the fishing rods, she couldn't resist stealing them.

The sisters had hidden the rods in the mangroves. They planned to pick them up another day.

Solution to
The Case of the Brain Game

The children were asked to write nine three-letter, common body parts.

When Mrs. Taylor read Chester's and Cindy's lists, Tyrone looked over her shoulder. He learned which word Cindy had missed.

After the game Encyclopedia looked at Cindy's list. The first eight body parts she had written were leg, eye, ear, arm, jaw, rib, lip, and toe.

The ninth body part was at the bottom of her list. Encyclopedia knew it had been given her by Tyrone.

He had blown a bubble-gum bubble.

The ninth word was *gum*—the kind that surrounds your teeth.

Shamed, Cindy gave Chester her prize.

Solution to
The Case of Black Jack's Treasure

Location of Treasure buried ten feet from young Tree by me this twenty-fifth January 1763. Black Jack Lefever

Wilford Wiggins had to prove that the tree was the one mentioned in the ship's log by Black Jack Lefever.

The pirate had written that he had carved his name on a small tree as a guide to where the treasure was buried.

Naturally, after more than a century the tree would have grown tall. Wilford figured that Black Jack's name would now be high above the ground.

So he carved BLACK JACK LEFEVER twenty feet up the trunk.

That was Wilford's mistake!

As Encyclopedia knew, a tree grows higher mainly from the top. A mark put on the trunk of a tree will stay about the same height above the ground no matter how tall the tree grows.

Solution to
The Case of the Missing Shopping Bag

The telephone call Mrs. Ryan made was not about returning the gray skirt. Just Skirts, the store where she bought the skirt, was closed for inventory.

So she was talking about something else when she said, "I've decided to get rid of the gray. I don't like it. . . . No, the length is all right."

Encyclopedia realized she was talking

about her *hair*. She was making an appointment with the beauty parlor in the shopping center!

That's where the boys found her.

She said she had put the gray skirt in Ike's shopping bag by mistake and moved it from the front door to her bedroom closet.

Ike returned the pamphlet to Hewitt just in time!

Solution to
The Case of the Disgusting Sneakers

The thief was Ann, who knew too much. She told Tessie Bottoms that someone had stolen Phoebe's right sneaker while Phoebe was clipping her "toenails."

That was her slip.

Only the thief, having seen Phoebe in the garage, could have known she was clipping her toenails, not her fingernails.

Phoebe had told Ann merely that she was clipping her "nails."

When Encyclopedia pointed out her mistake, Ann confessed. She gave Phoebe her third prize, a can of foot powder.

"Wait till next year," Phoebe vowed.

Solution to
The Case of the Smugglers' Secret

The word *copy* tipped off Encyclopedia.
If the boxes were searched in the United States, the police would think the clay pots were only cheap copies.

The pots were actually three thousand years old and worth a fortune.

Had the pots really been meant for sale in Spain as cheap copies, *copy* would not have been written in English. It would have been written in *Spanish,* as were the fake addresses on the boxes.

Chief Brown checked. The pots had been stolen from a museum in South America. They were to be sold in the United States to a dishonest dealer, who would rub the word *copy* off each pot. He would then sell the pots at their true worth to rich, unsuspecting U.S. customers.

The smugglers were arrested.

ABOUT THE AUTHOR

DONALD J. SOBOL is the creator of the highly acclaimed Encyclopedia Brown solve-it-yourself series. In addition, he has written the "Wacky" series and the "Encyclopedia Brown Record Books." His awards include the Pacific Northwest Reader's Choice Award for *Encyclopedia Brown Keeps the Peace* and a special Edgar from the Mystery Writers of America for his contribution to mystery writing in the United States.

A native of New York, Donald J. Sobol now lives in Florida with his wife.

ABOUT THE ILLUSTRATOR

GAIL OWENS is a well-known children's book illustrator living and working in Rock Tavern, New York. Among the many books she has illustrated are *Encyclopedia Brown and the Case of the Mysterious Handprints* and *Encyclopedia Brown and the Case of the Treasure Hunt*, both available from Bantam Books.